ALLOSAURUS

PTERANODON

CORYTHOSAURUS

APATOSAURUS

DIMETRODON

ANKYLOSAURUS

TRACHODON

TYRANNOSAURUS REX

STEGOSAURUS

TRICERATOPS

JANE YOLEN has written more than two hundred books for children and adults, including *Owl Moon*, which was awarded the Caldecott Medal. Her long list of honors includes the World Fantasy Award, the Regina Medal, the Kerlan Award, the Christopher Medal, the Nebula, and the Golden Kite Award.

She lives with her husband in western Massachusetts and in St. Andrews, Scotland. They have three grown children and three grandchildren.

MARK TEAGUE has delighted young readers with more than twenty picture books, and he has written many of them himself, including the popular *Pigsty*, *Baby Tamer*, and *One Halloween Night*. He is also the illustrator of Cynthia Rylant's beloved Poppleton series for beginning readers. Mark and his wife live in Coxsackie, New York, with their young daughter, Lily, who had a great time watching her dad paint the dinosaurs in this book.

JANE YOLEN

How Do Dinosaurs Say Good Night?

Illustrated by

MARK TEAGUE

THE BLUE SKY PRESS
An Imprint of Scholastic Inc. • New York

BOK 1090

THE BLUE SKY PRESS

ISBN 0-439-66528-0

This book was originally published in hardcover by Blue Sky Press in 2000.

12 11 10 9 8 7 6 5 4 3 2 1 4 5 6 7 8 9/0

Printed in Mexico 49

First printing, April 2004

This edition published in 2004 by Scholastic Inc.
exclusively for Hallmark Cards, Inc.
www.hallmark.com

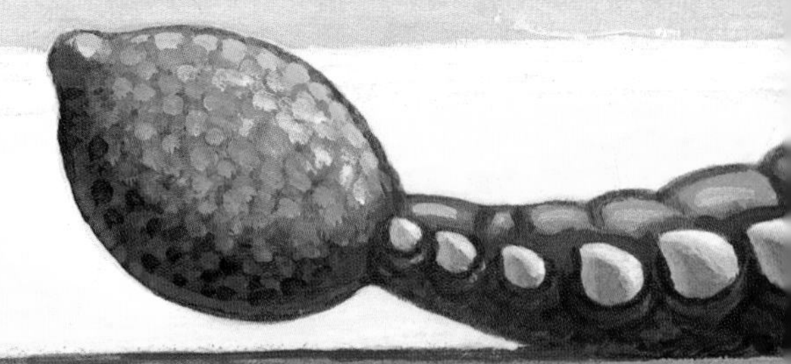

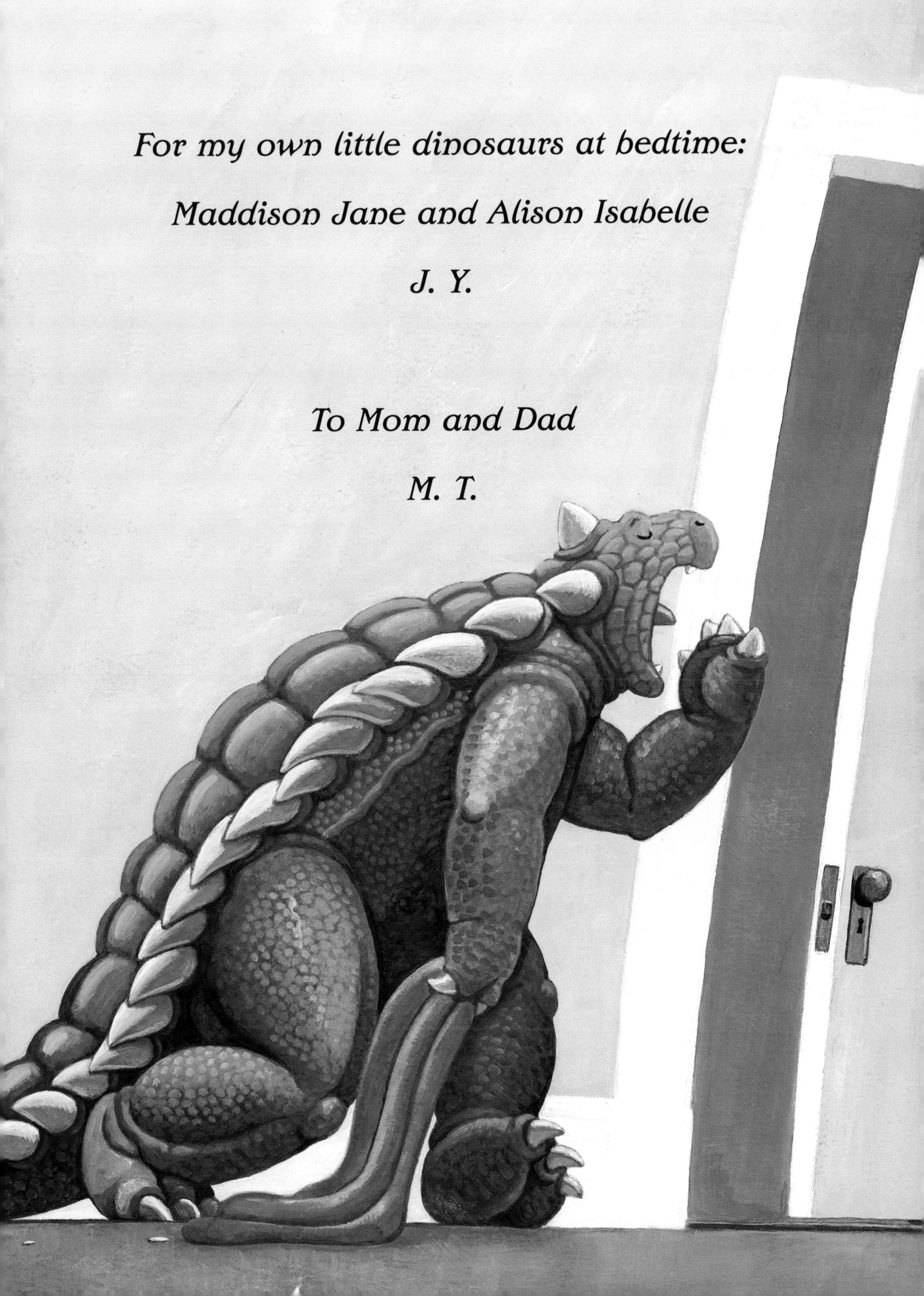

For my own little dinosaurs at bedtime:

Maddison Jane and Alison Isabelle

J. Y.

To Mom and Dad

M. T.

How does
a dinosaur say
good night
when Papa
comes in
to turn off
the light?

TYRANNOSAURUS REX

STEGOSAURUS

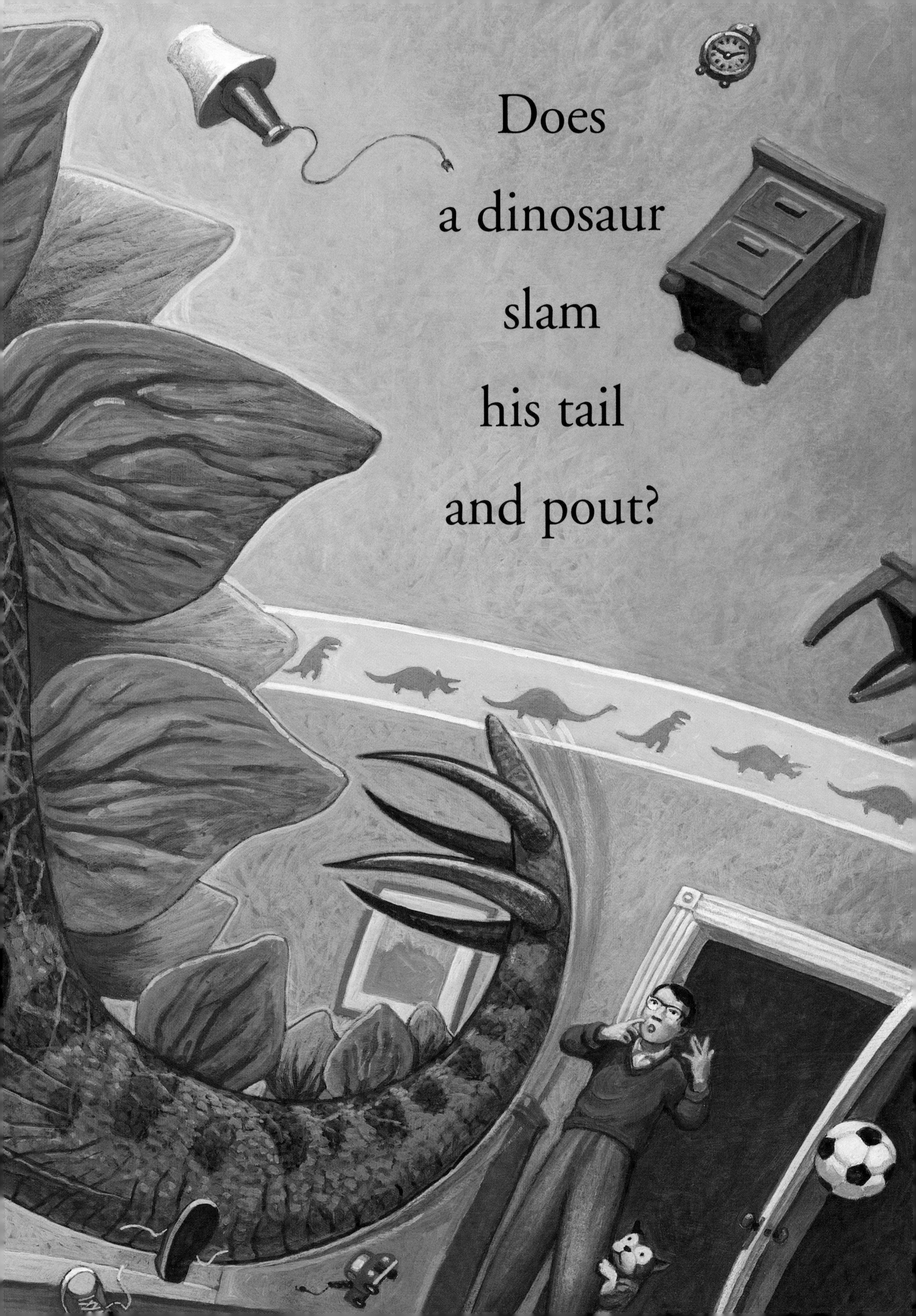

Does
a dinosaur
slam
his tail
and pout?

PTERANODON

Does he throw
his teddy bear
all about?

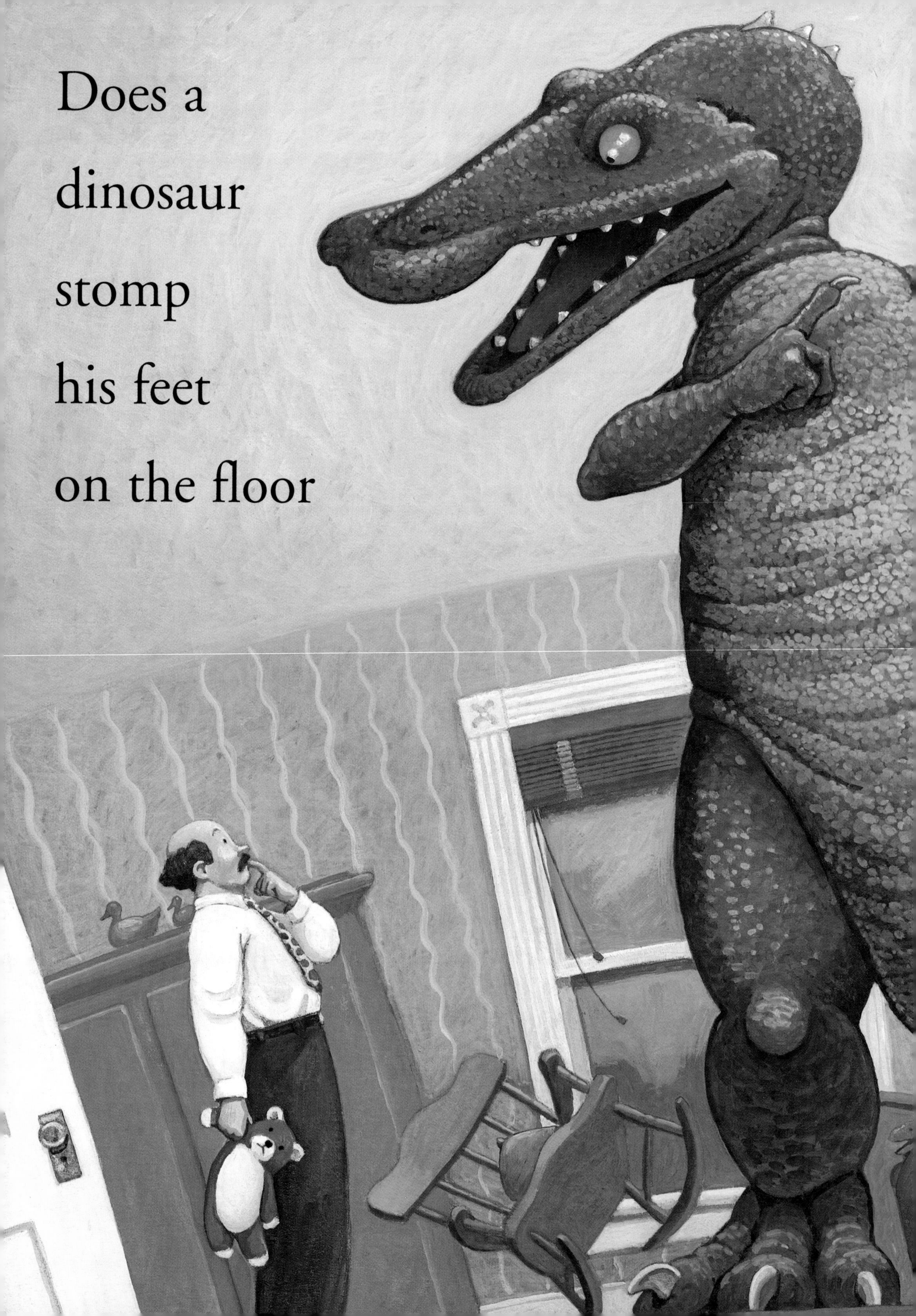

Does a
dinosaur
stomp
his feet
on the floor

and shout:
"I want
to hear
one book
more!"?

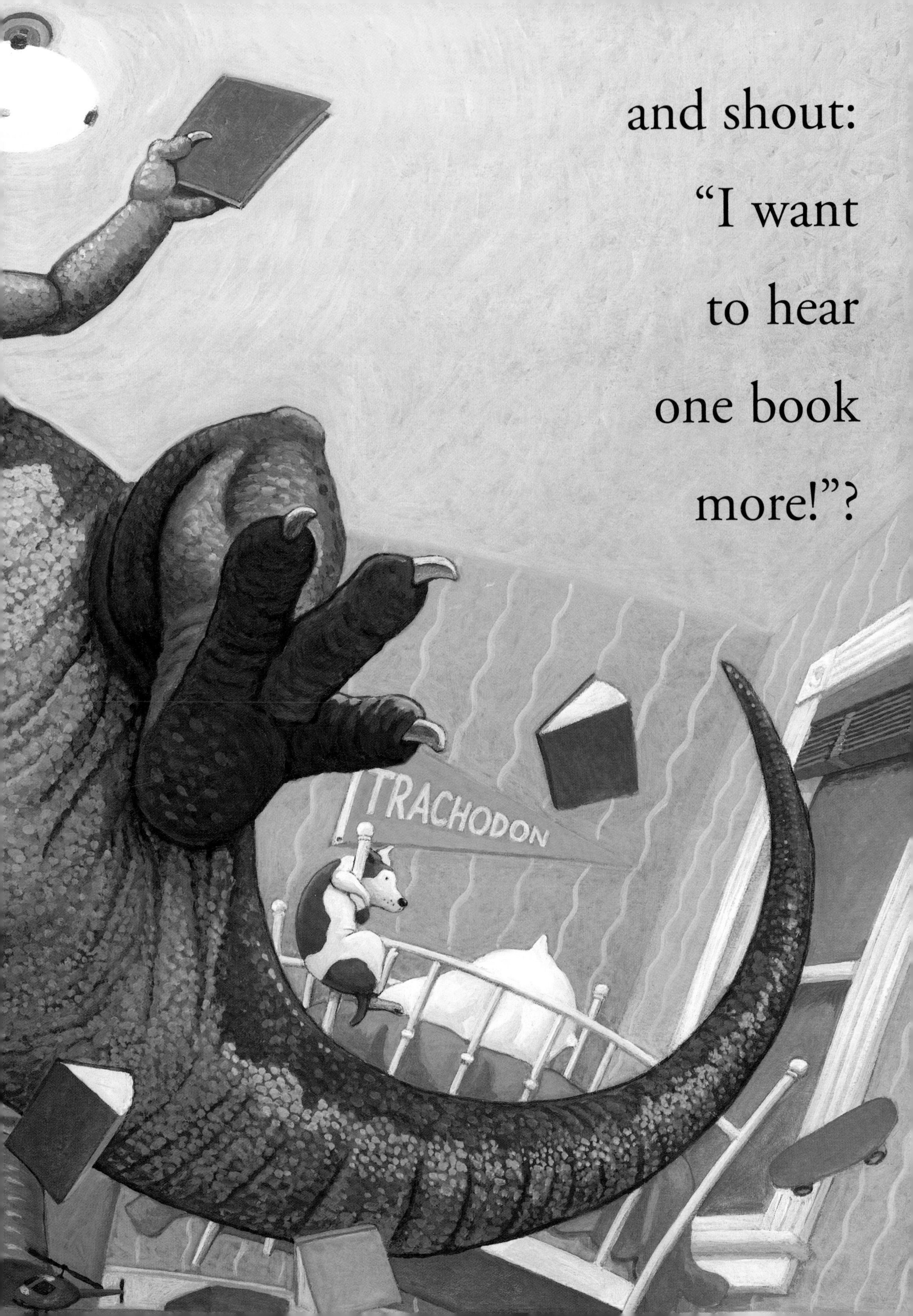

DOES

A DINOSAUR

ROAR?

TRICERATOPS

How does a dinosaur say good night
when *Mama* comes in
to turn off the light?

Does he swing his neck
from side to side?

Does he up
and demand
a piggyback ride?

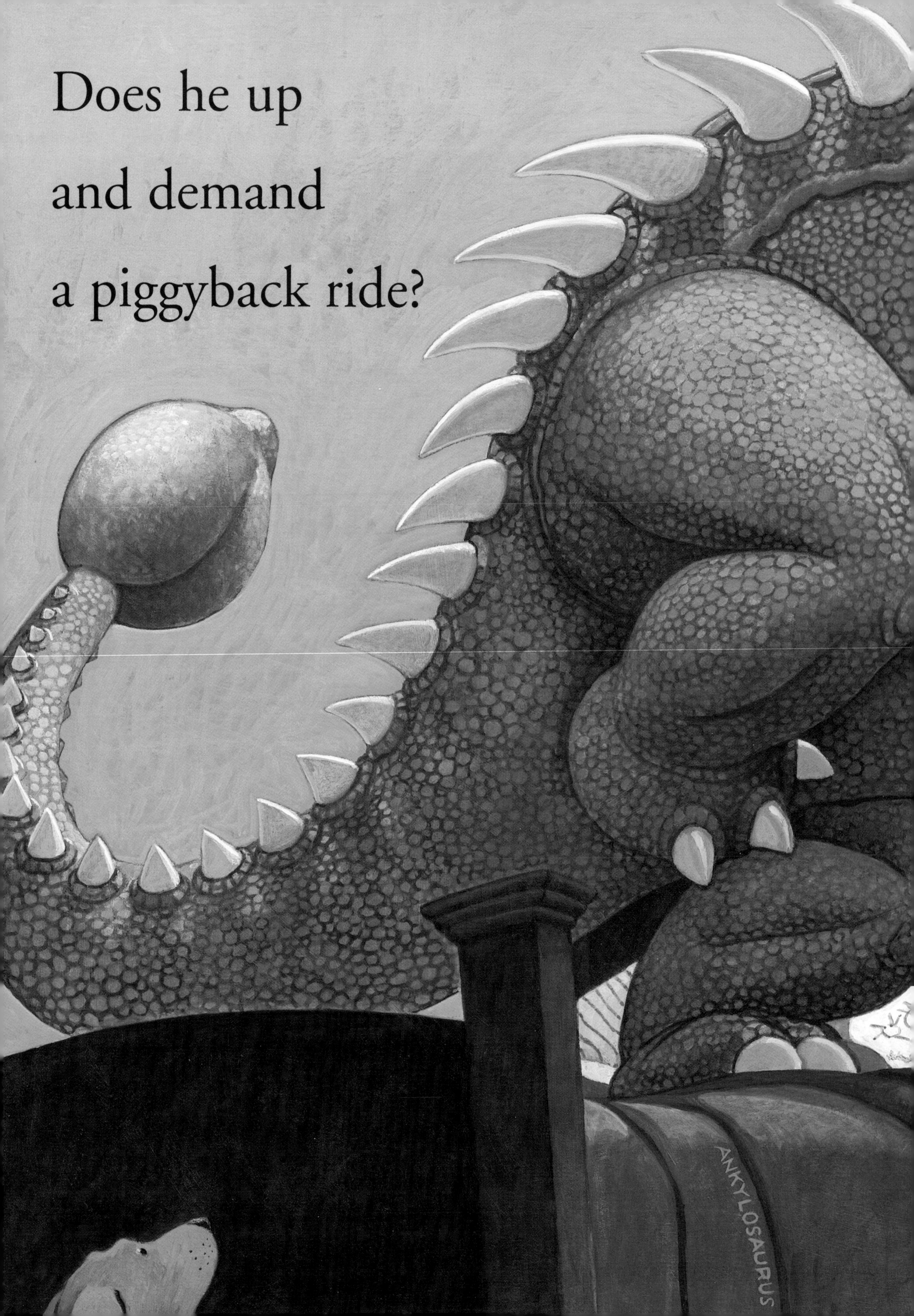

Does he mope,

does he moan,

does he sulk,

does he sigh?

Does he fall on the top

of his covers and cry?

No, dinosaurs don't.
They don't even try.
They give
a big kiss.

T-REX

STEGOSAURUS

They turn out
the light.

They tuck in
their tails.
They whisper,
“Good night!”

They give
a big hug,
then give
one kiss
more.

Good night.

Good night, little dinosaur.

Allosaurus

Pteranodon

Corythosaurus

Apatosaurus

Dimetrodon

Ankylosaurus

Trachodon

Tyrannosaurus Rex

Stegosaurus

Triceratops